MR. MEN

Ready, Steady, Bake!

Roger Hargreaves

Original concept by
Roger Hargreaves

Written and illustrated by
Adam Hargreaves

It was the big event of the year.
The Summer Fete Baking Competition!

This year Mr Clever was in charge.

And one of Mr Clever's jobs was to choose the
competition judges. But who should they be?

Everyone else was very busy practising
their baking.

Like Little Miss Busy.
She practised.
And practised.
And practised.

What a lot of cakes!

Baking is a very precise type of cooking and Little Miss Neat made sure that she very carefully measured and weighed all the ingredients for her bake.

She had measuring spoons and measuring cups and measuring jugs and lots of weighing scales.

And because she was so neat and careful and precise she made one small, but perfect, jam tart.

Mr Rush, on the other hand, was in too much of a rush to bother measuring anything.

Or bother weighing anything.

Or bother mixing anything properly.

And, he was in far too much of a rush to leave his cake in the oven long enough to cook.

It was not a delicious cake.

It was a mess!

But not as big a mess as Mr Worry's kitchen!

Little Miss Naughty had sneakily loosened the lid on his food mixer.

Oh dear. Pink icing everywhere.

What a worry!

Mr Silly decided not to bake something sweet.

He made a sausage roll …

... all the way down
the hill!

The day before the competition everyone went to the shop to buy all the things they needed.

Now, to bake something tasty you need lots of tasty ingredients.

Mr Perfect bought: Strawberries, chocolate, vanilla, cream.

YUMMY!

Mr Mean's list, on the other hand, was not so exciting. He bought one currant.

Only one currant for his currant bun!

How mean!

And then it was the day of the Summer Fete.
In the baking tent, everyone waited nervously
behind their cooking stations.

"Ready! Steady! Bake!" cried Mr Clever.

And then they were off. Mixing and beating and rolling and blending and kneading as quickly as they could.

They only had two hours to finish their entries.

Poor Mr Slow.

It took him one hour to break one egg!

Mr Impossible really wanted to impress the judges.
He baked an upside-down cake.

Upside down!

I'm not sure Mr Forgetful is going to win any prizes this year.

He forgot to turn his oven on.

His cake was very runny!

And that wasn't the only disaster …

Little Miss Whoops tripped over her rolling pin and dropped her chocolate cupcakes.

WHOOPS!

And Mr Wrong put too much baking powder in his cake mix.

There would be no prizes for Mr Muddle's entry, either.
He was trying to bake a loaf of bread, but muddled up
flour and flower.

Little Miss Naughty made a custard pie.
And can you guess what she did with it?

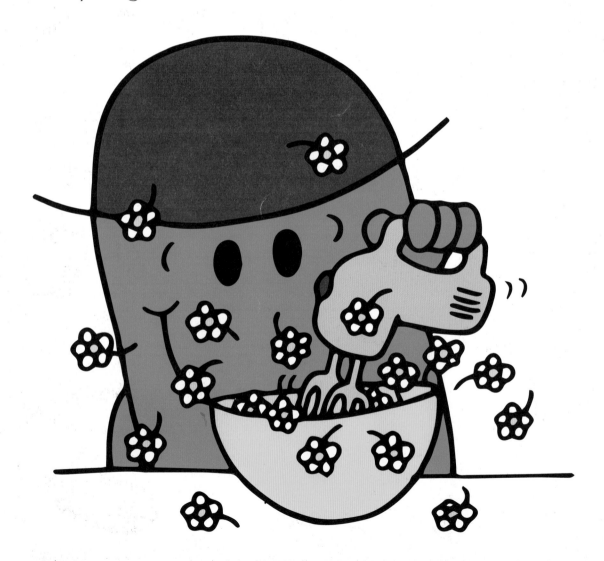

That's right!

Mr Skinny baked one tiny biscuit, just the right size for his tiny appetite.

And Little Miss Splendid made a splendid cake.

It was so big Mr Strong had to help her carry it up to the judging table.

What a show off!

What a lot of entries there were to judge. Cakes and muffins and tarts and biscuits and bread and pies and pastries.

Mr Clever had chosen two judges who know an awful lot about food.

Everyone left the tent while the judges considered the entries and decided who had won a prize.

But when they were called back in for the prize-giving, the table of entries was bare.

Not a cake or a biscuit or a pie was left.

It had all disappeared.
Every crumb,
Every morsel,
Every scrap!

Have you guessed who Mr Clever had chosen to judge?

That's right!

Mr Greedy and Little Miss Greedy.

And all the food had disappeared into their tummies!

And what very big tummies they were.

Mr Greedy and Little Miss Greedy had gobbled up the food so fast that they had no idea who had baked what.

Except for Little Miss Naughty's custard pie.
Mr Clever knew exactly what had happened to that!

All they could do was award first prize to everybody.

Which was an unexpected surprise for Mr Forgetful!

Maybe Mr Clever is not quite as clever as he thinks he is.

Choosing Mr Greedy and Little Miss Greedy to be judges is what you might call ...

... a recipe for disaster!